BILLY'S BUCKET

First published in Great Britain in 2003 by The Bodley Head,
an imprint of Random House Children's Books

First U.S. edition 2003

Library of Congress Cataloging-in-Publication Data

Gray, Kes.
Billy's bucket / Kes Gray ; Garry Parsons. — 1st U.S. ed.
p. cm.
Summary: Despite his parents' protests, Billy wants nothing for his birthday but a very
special bucket and all goes well until the bucket is borrowed without his permission.
ISBN 0-7636-2127-7
[1. Pails—Fiction. 2. Imagination—Fiction. 3. Birthdays—Fiction.] I. Parsons, Garry, ill. II. Title.
PZ7.G77428 Bi 2003
[E]—dc21 2002034870

Printed in Singapore

This book was typeset in Jacoby Light.
The illustrations were done in acrylic.

Candlewick Press
2067 Massachusetts Avenue
Cambridge, Massachusetts 02140

visit us at www.candlewick.com

For Mum and Dad — K. G.

For Ange, Pat, Charmz,
and Austen — G. P.

BILLY'S BUCKET

Kes Gray

illustrated by

Garry Parsons

CANDLEWICK PRESS
CAMBRIDGE, MASSACHUSETTS

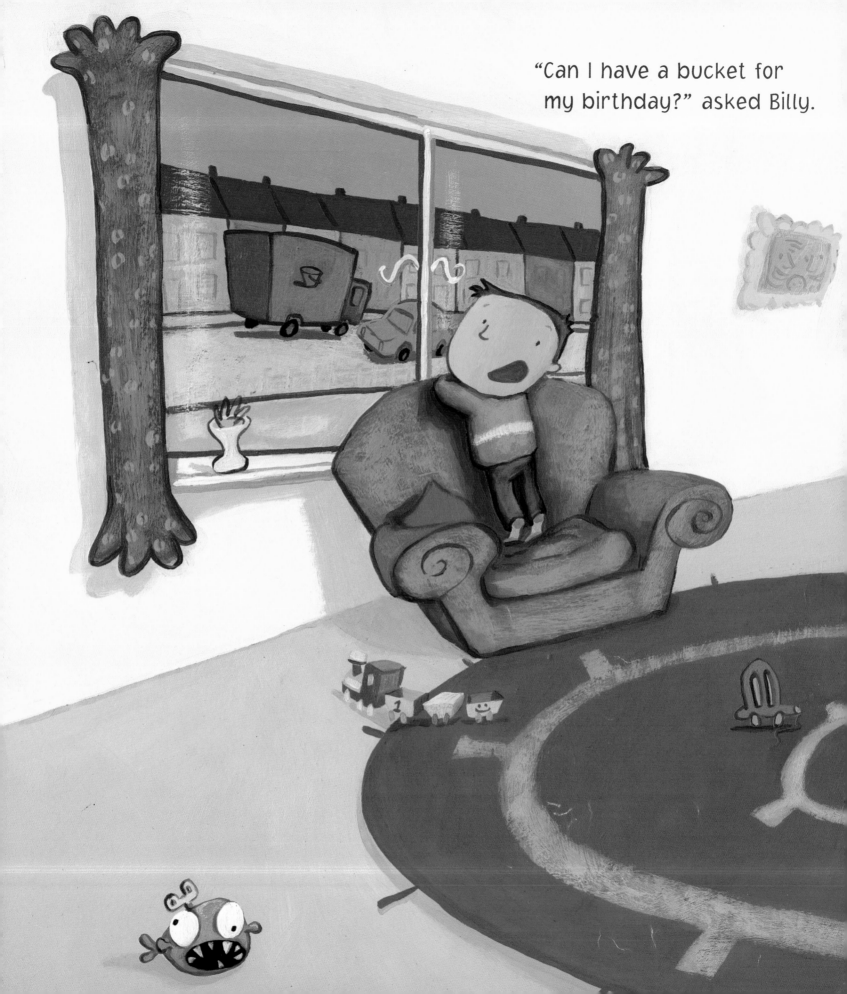

"Can I have a bucket for my birthday?" asked Billy.

Billy's dad looked up from his newspaper.

"A bucket? You don't want a bucket for your birthday. No one gets a bucket for his birthday."

"Why not?" asked Billy.

"Because, Billy," explained his mom, "buckets are . . . well, buckets are far too BUCKETTY to be a birthday present."

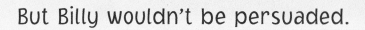

But Billy wouldn't be persuaded.

"**Please** can I have a bucket?"
he asked.

"How about
a bike?"
said his dad.

"Or some new
sneakers,"
said his mom.

"Or a computer
game."

"I want a bucket,"
said Billy.

"All right," sighed
Billy's dad. "You can
have a bucket for
your birthday."

"Yippee!"
shouted Billy.

The next day,
Billy and his mom and
dad went to Buckets Я Us.
There were buckets of buckets at
Buckets Я Us: rubber buckets, plastic buckets,
metal buckets, garden buckets, farm buckets,
builders' buckets, beach buckets, and even soccer buckets.

Billy's mom and dad followed Billy up and down every single aisle.
"What kind of bucket are you looking for?" they asked.

"I don't know," said Billy, "but I'll know it when I see it."

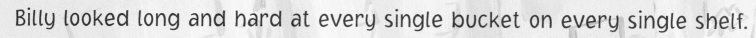

Billy looked long and hard at every single bucket on every single shelf.
"There it is," he shouted. **"That's the one I want,**
right there — 19 shelves up, 78 across from the left!"

Billy's mom and dad got someone to help them.

"They all look the same to me,"
said the salesclerk doubtfully.

"No, that one's special,"
said Billy excitedly.

When Billy got home, he ran straight into the kitchen and filled his bucket with water.

"Cool!" said Billy, peering inside his bucket.

"I can see a rock pool with crabs and seaweed and little shrimpy things!"

"Of course you can, Billy," agreed his dad.

"Of course you did, Billy." His mom smiled.

"Guess what I just saw!"
exclaimed Billy, sitting down for his birthday dinner. "I saw a stingray, some clown fish, a bunch of barracuda, and a mermaid, I think, but it might have been a big herring."

"Of course you did, Billy." His dad chuckled.

"What's in your bucket at the moment, Billy?" His dad chuckled again.

"Two submarines and a sardine," said Billy.

"What's in your bucket now, Billy?" His mom giggled.

"Seven sea lions and a walrus," said Billy.

"Of course!" his parents exclaimed.

That night, Billy was still staring into his bucket.

Billy's dad nudged his wife and winked. "Billy, is it okay if we borrow your bucket to mix up some paint tomorrow?"

Billy shook his head. "No, it isn't. There are dolphins in my bucket right now. You must **never** borrow my bucket."

Billy's mom waited a few moments and winked at her husband. "Billy, is it okay if we borrow your bucket to water the roses tomorrow?"

Billy frowned. "There are two scuba divers in my bucket right now. You must **never ever** borrow my bucket."

Billy's dad just smiled and waited a few more moments. "Billy, is it okay if I borrow your bucket to wash the car tomorrow?"

Billy looked up from his bucket and sighed. "No, it isn't okay. There's a coral reef in my bucket right now.

You must never **ever** **ever** borrow my bucket!"

"What an imagination!" exclaimed Billy's mom and dad.
"But it's time for bed!"

Billy put his bucket away and went upstairs.

"Thanks for a great birthday!" he called.

"And the best present in the world!"

When Billy woke up the next morning, he got dressed quickly and ran downstairs to play with his bucket.

But it wasn't there.

By the time Billy found his dad, he was too late!

"I told you not to borrow my bucket," said Billy.

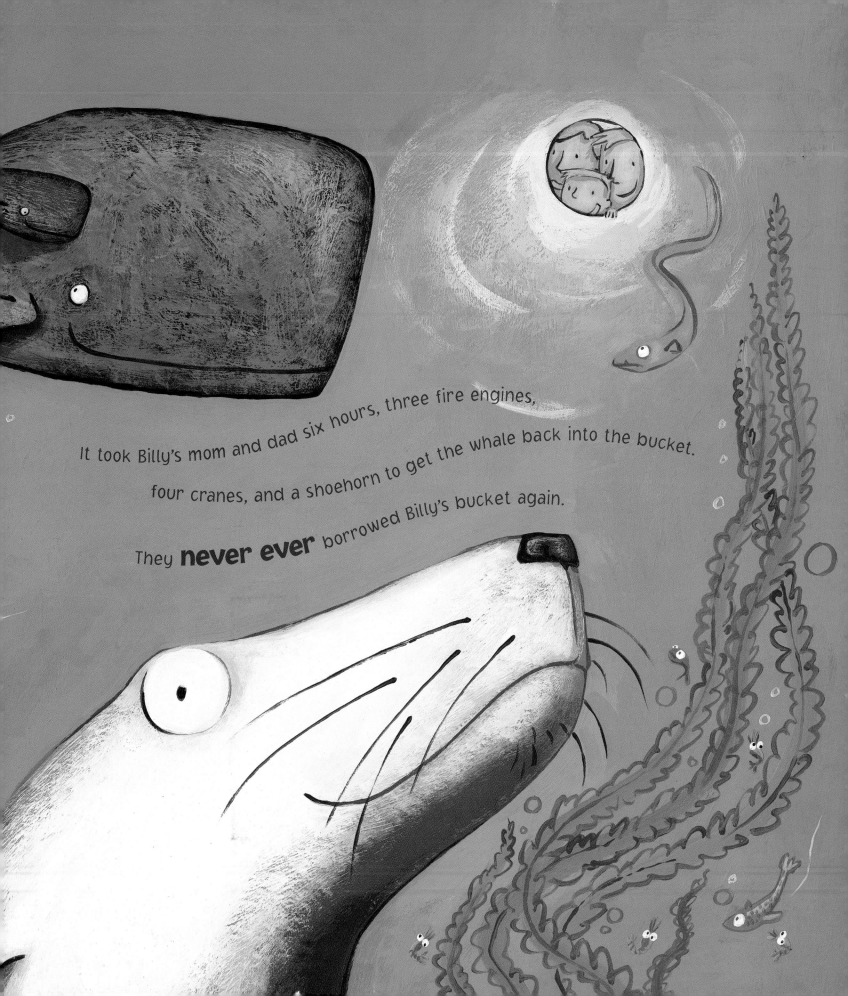

It took Billy's mom and dad six hours, three fire engines, four cranes, and a shoehorn to get the whale back into the bucket.

They **never ever** borrowed Billy's bucket again.